Jayda
the Snowboarding
Fairy

Join the **Rainbow Magic Reading Challenge!**

Read the story and collect your fairy points to climb the
Reading Rainbow at the back of the book.

This book is worth 1 star.

ORCHARD BOOKS

First published in Great Britain in 2021 by The Watts Publishing Group

1 3 5 7 9 10 8 6 4 2

© 2021 Rainbow Magic Limited.
© 2021 HIT Entertainment Limited.
Illustrations © 2021 The Watts Publishing Group Limited.

HIT entertainment

The moral rights of the author and illustrator have been asserted.

A CIP catalogue record for this book is available from the British Library.

ISBN 978 1 40836 457 4

Printed and bound in Great Britain by Clays Ltd, Elcograf S.p.A

MIX
Paper from
responsible sources
FSC® C104740
FSC
www.fsc.org

The paper and board used in this book are made from wood from responsible sources.

Orchard Books
An imprint of Hachette Children's Group
Part of The Watts Publishing Group Limited
Carmelite House, 50 Victoria Embankment, London EC4Y 0DZ

An Hachette UK Company
www.hachette.co.uk
www.hachettechildrens.co.uk

Jayda
the Snowboarding
Fairy

By Daisy Meadows

ORCHARD

www.orchardseriesbooks.co.uk

Jack Frost's Ode

Each goody-goody fairy pest
Says 'Never cheat' and 'Try your best'.
Their words should end up in the bin.
To be the best you have to win!

I'll steal and cheat to find a way
Of winning every game I play,
And when the world is at my feet
They'll see it's always best to cheat!

Contents

Chapter One: Jealous Jack   9

Chapter Two: Goblin Snowball   19

Chapter Three: Mountain Accident   31

Chapter Four: Hot-air Rescue   39

Chapter Five: Snowball Surprise   53

Chapter Six: The Big Air   63

Chapter One
Jealous Jack

"WOW!"

Rachel Walker whooped as a snowboarder sped down the biggest slope in the snowboard park.

"Do you think we'll ever be able to do that?" said her best friend, Kirsty Tate.

"I hope so," said Rachel, crossing her

fingers. "It looks like lots of fun."

It was Rachel and Kirsty's third day in Dewbelle Resort in the Mistfall Mountains. Together with a group of children from various schools, they had been taking part in the Gold Medal Games since last summer. The snowboarding competition was the last event of the season.

"Don't worry," said their snowboarding instructor, Kim. "We were all beginners once. The best thing you can do is relax and have fun."

The board park was next to the main ski slope, and it was filled with snowboarders doing the best kicks, flicks and tricks the girls had ever seen. They were sliding on slopes, half pipes and even picnic tables.

"Awesome!" exclaimed Valentina, who had won the skiing gold medal the day before.

She was gazing at a snowboarder who had just done a full somersault in mid-air. He was dressed in ice blue, and his white helmet had an ice-blue lightning bolt on its side. His board was also white and blue, and it was decorated with pink and yellow flowers.

"That's Lightning Jack," said Joe, a boy from Kirsty's school. "He's amazing. I've been watching him."

Rachel and Kirsty exchanged a worried glance. They knew that Lightning Jack was Jack Frost in disguise. After stealing the magical belongings of the Gold Medal Games Fairies, he had tried to win every Gold Medal competition by cheating. The snowboarding round was his last chance.

"It's horrible seeing Jack Frost with Jayda's snowboard," Kirsty whispered to Rachel.

The girls had helped three of their friends the Gold Medal Games Fairies to get their special objects back. Jayda the Snowboarding Fairy was the only one still waiting.

"Hopefully we can stop him and get Jayda's board back in time," said Rachel. "But first, we've got a few things to learn about snowboarding."

"Gather round, everyone," said Kim. "I'm going to start by teaching you a few snowboarding basics. First, you'll attach yourself to your snowboard by putting your feet into the bindings. Then you'll learn how to stand and slide. This afternoon, you'll get to try a few jumps. Then tomorrow, you will all compete in a big air for the final gold medal."

"What's a big air?" Rachel asked.

"It's what we call a jumping
competition," Kim explained. "You'll
launch off a slope, do a simple trick in
the air and then land. It's looks super
cool."

As she spoke, Jack Frost flew into the
air, twirled around and landed cleanly on
a nearby slope.

"Just like that," said Kim, laughing.
"Hey, come back!"

She beckoned to three boys who had
edged away while she was talking. They
were standing at the top of a slope.
Under their helmets and goggles, the girls
couldn't tell who they were.

"You're not ready for that," Kim called.

WHOOOSH! The boys threw
themselves down the slope in a tangle of
boards, boots and big feet. They landed in

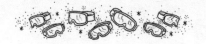

a heap, yelling and groaning.

"Ha!" shouted Jack Frost, pointing at them and laughing. "I'm the best and you're all rubbish. I'll win the gold medal. Me! Lightning Jack of the Frost Academy!"

He looked around at the others in the board park with a sneer. The three boys limped back to join the group. They passed Rachel and Kirsty, grumbling to each other.

"It was all your stupid fault," one of them squawked.

Kirsty gasped.

"That was a goblin voice," she whispered.

"Lightning Jack is wrong," Kim was saying. "Snowboarding isn't about beating everyone else and laughing at them. It's about being the best you can be and having fun."

She hopped on her board and stood at the top of a half pipe. She dropped into a run and launched into a jump that seemed to last for ever. Many of the

snowboarders in the park stopped and cheered as she landed and raised her hands above her head.

"She's amazing!" whooped Lenny, who was from the same school as Valentina. "Look how much everyone loves her!"

The girls saw Jack Frost scowl.

"I think he heard that," said Rachel in a low voice.

"He looks jealous," said Kirsty. "I hope he doesn't do something naughty."

Chapter Two
Goblin Snowball

Jack Frost turned his back on the gold medal group and headed towards the other side of the park.

"Maybe he isn't going to do anything," said Kirsty hopefully.

"He doesn't need to," said Rachel with a sigh. "Have you noticed how many things are going wrong?"

Kirsty looked around. Lenny's boots
had just come undone for the third time.
Three of the students had loose bindings,
and one girl's board had a bent edge.

"As long as Jack Frost has Jayda's
board, things will go wrong for the gold

medal snowboarders," said Rachel.

"OK, everyone," said Kim, when she had sorted out the loose boots and bindings. "The first thing is to figure out if you're regular or goofy."

Everyone looked confused, and Kim let out a small laugh.

"We're not goofy!" exclaimed the shortest goblin in an offended voice.

"It's just a way of describing which is your leading foot," said Kim. "If you start with your left foot forward, we say you're a regular snowboarder. If you prefer to start with your right foot forward, we say you're a goofy snowboarder."

Everyone giggled as they worked out what they were.

"Next, heel slides and toe slides," said Kim. "Remember, it's all about balance and confidence. You can do it!"

They practised hard, and although little things kept going wrong, no one gave up. It was so much fun sliding on the snow. Soon, they were all doing what Kim called a 'falling leaf' – sliding from one side of the slope to the other, first on the

heel side and then on the toe side of
their boards.

"This is not as easy as it
looks," said Kirsty, panting
and wobbling.

"I don't feel much
like a falling leaf,"
said Lenny as he
landed on his
bottom.

"More like a sinking stone."

"This is boring," the shortest goblin complained. "We want to learn how to jump."

"If you don't learn the basics, you could have a serious injury," said Kim.

They went back to the top of the slope to practise the falling leaf again. But Rachel lost her balance and her snowboard slipped. Suddenly she was plunging straight down the slope, speeding towards a picnic table.

"Rachel!" cried Kirsty. "Look out!"

Rachel's knees wobbled and she fell, but kept sliding. With a gasp, she crossed her arms in front of her face . . . and gently bumped against one of the table legs.

"What happened?" she murmured, lowering her arms.

"Snowboarding magic," said a calm voice.

Rachel looked up and saw Jayda the Snowboarding Fairy. She was sitting on little ridge of ice that had formed under the table top.

"Hi, Jayda," said Rachel with a smile. "It's really great to see you."

Jayda was wearing blue trousers, a multi-coloured jacket and a blue helmet with her wand tucked into it. Her curly brown hair fell around her

shoulders as she leaned forwards to smile at Rachel.

"Hey, Rachel," she said. "How are you doing?"

"Fine, because of you," said Rachel. "Thank you for slowing me down."

"No problem," said Jayda, waving her hand. "Are you having fun?"

"It's amazing," said Rachel. "If only
Jack Frost wasn't trying to spoil things."

"It's very uncool of him," said Jayda.
"But it'll be fine."

"How can you be so sure?" Rachel
asked.

"Because you and Kirsty are on my
side," said Jayda.

She fluttered down and slipped into
Rachel's jacket pocket. Smiling, Rachel
unclicked from her board and crawled
out from under the table. Kirsty slid to
her side.

"Are you OK?" she asked.

"Better than OK," whispered Rachel,
smiling. "Jayda's here."

The girls found a quiet corner of the
board park and knelt down to talk to the
little fairy.

"How are things in Fairyland?" Kirsty asked.

"Pretty cool," said Jayda. "Soraya and I have organised a Snow Fun Day for the fairies. The palace is surrounded by snow."

"What a great idea," said Rachel.

"But I can't join in without my snowboard," said Jayda with a longing sigh. "And without it, no one will enjoy the final of the gold medal games."

"We'll do everything we can to help," said Kirsty.

"I'm here with a message from the queen," Jayda said. "She has invited you both to visit her. Will you come?"

"Of course we will," said Rachel.

Jayda reached for her wand, but before she could do anything, there was a cry behind them. They turned and gasped. The impatient goblins had once again started down a slope that was too steep for them. Flailing wildly, they jumped, hurtled over the fence and rolled down the hill towards Dewbelle.

"They're turning into a giant goblin snowball," Kirsty cried. "Someone has to stop them!"

"Quick, under the picnic table," said Rachel.

She pulled Kirsty with her and Jayda lifted her wand. A tiny, fizzing glow of light, as bright as a sparkler, zoomed towards them. It whizzed around them, faster and faster, until it was a mere blur. The girls felt themselves spinning and dwindling, and knew that they were shrinking to fairy size. Their delicate wings unfurled.

"Let's fly," said Jayda.

They zoomed out from under the table . . . into the scowling face of Jack Frost!

Chapter Three
Mountain Accident

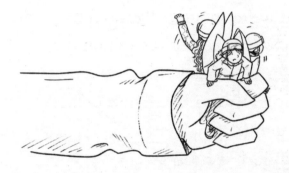

Jack Frost snatched the three fairies in his hand.

"Got you!" he hissed. "You're not spoiling my chances this time. You ruined the other competitions for me, but now I'm going to lock you up so you can't stick your tiny little noses in."

He plucked Jayda's wand from her hand as if he were picking a daisy. Then he dropped them all into a bobble hat, and clutched it in his fist.

"We're trapped," said Rachel with a groan.

"And we're moving," said Jayda.

Kirsty tugged at the wool, tearing the fibres so that she could peep through.

"He's snowboarding after the goblins," she said. "We're heading towards the resort."

"In that case, we're going in the right direction," said Jayda, lying back with her hands behind her head.

The hat swung to and fro. They heard the swoosh of the snowboard stopping, and then Jack Frost jumped off his board.

"The goblins are heading towards the ice skating rink," said Kirsty, still peering through the hat.

The goblin snowball hurtled through the doors and onto the oval ice rink, where it hit a side wall and broke apart. The goblins flailed across the ice, their feet still clamped into their snowboards.

"Come here, you blibbering idiots," Jack Frost raged.

The goblins squawked in alarm, kicked off their boards and scrambled towards Jack Frost. He glared at each of them as they ran past him. Then he turned and followed them outside.

"In this hat are three fairies who have been trying to stop me," he told them in an icy voice. "Take them deep into the Mistfall Mountains, and throw this wand into a ravine."

Rachel and Kirsty exchanged alarmed looks.

"We're trapped!" said Kirsty.

The goblins walked for what felt like a long time. They took turns to swing the hat as they stomped along, and the fairies were flung on top of each other.

"It's lucky we don't get travel sick," said Kirsty, helping Rachel off Jayda for the sixth time.

Jayda closed her eyes.

"I'm just going to imagine I'm swinging in a hammock," she said. "The only trouble is, I might fall asleep."

"I have *never* met anyone as relaxed as you, Jayda," said Kirsty. "Aren't you worried at all?"

Jayda opened one eye for a moment and shrugged.

"Being stuck in a hat without a wand definitely makes things tricky," she said. "But I'm sure we'll think of something."

The goblins were talking about Dewbelle.

"The others said that it's haunted by the ghost of Spider Pickles," said the first goblin in a shaky voice.

"They made that up," scoffed the second goblin. "They just want us to fail because they lost Jack Frost's magical skis."

"I don't want to meet a g-g-ghost," said the third goblin.

"I've got an idea," Kirsty said suddenly.

She cupped her hands around her mouth and shouted as loud as she could,

"I am the Ghost of Knobbly Knee; set your little prisoners free!"

There was a loud squawk of fear, and then the hat went spinning through the air. They landed with a bump.

"Ouch!" cried Rachel.

"Quick, let's push our way out before the goblins pick us up again," said Kirsty.

She held up the floppy material of the hat to let Rachel and Jayda crawl out.

"Where *are* the goblins?" asked Rachel, fluttering above the snow.

Kirsty followed her out and gazed around. They were high in the mountains above Dewbelle, which was hidden by a misty cloud. She could see snow-tipped trees and distant mountain peaks. But there wasn't a goblin in sight.

"Where did they go?" asked Kirsty in amazement.

Jayda flew up and glided in small circles.

"Down there!" she exclaimed, pointing. "They've fallen into a ravine."

Chapter Four
Hot-air Rescue

The three goblins were trembling on a narrow, rocky ledge. The fairies zoomed down and fluttered in front of them.

"You poor things," said Rachel.

"Try not to be scared," said Kirsty, smiling at them. "We're going to help you to get down."

Rachel glanced up. The top of the ravine was several metres away.

"I'm not good with climbing," wailed the goblin on the left.

"I'm not good with heights," the one in the middle squawked.

"I want to go back to Goblin Grotto," whined the goblin on the right.

"Take it easy," said Jayda, perching on the ledge. "I can get you out of here and send you straight home to Goblin Grotto. But I'm going to need my wand . . ."

At once, the middle goblin held out her

tiny wand in the palm of his shaking, bony hand. Jayda took it and spoke the words of a spell:

*"Rescue those who chose to roam,
And carry each one safely home."*

A shining cord of pure light shot out of the tip of her wand, coiling itself around and around until it had formed a basket large enough for the goblins. Next, a bubble inflated from the wand's tip, swelling until it was even bigger than the basket. Ribbons of light tied the basket underneath the bubble.

"It's a magical hot-air balloon," Rachel exclaimed.

"This will carry you home in style," said Jayda. "Hop in."

The basket hovered steadily in front of the ledge. One by one, the goblins jumped into it.

"There's a box of fresh bogmallows in there for the journey," said Jayda. "Enjoy your trip."

The goblins dived into the bottom of the basket. The sound of them squabbling over the bogmallows faded as the hot-air balloon carried them away from the Mistfall Mountains.

"Well done, Jayda," said Kirsty. "But why didn't you just magic them straight to Goblin Grotto?"

"Sometimes enjoying the journey is just as important as getting where you want to go," said Jayda. "It's the same with snowboarding. The fun is in getting down the mountain, not arriving at the bottom."

Rachel gave a sudden exclamation.

"I've just remembered that the queen is waiting for us," she said. "We need to get to Fairyland."

"That's true," said Jayda. "And this time the journey needs to be as quick as possible."

She waved her wand, and sparkling fairy dust swirled around them. For a few seconds it was like being inside a whirlwind of glittering diamonds. Then the sparkles cleared, and they were flying high above the pink Fairyland Palace.

Everything around it was covered in
a thick layer of powdery snow that
glittered in the sunlight. They flew down
to the entrance, where they saw an old
friend.

"Bertram!" exclaimed Kirsty, hugging
the frog footman. "It's great to see you."

"Welcome back,"
said Bertram with
a wide smile.

He was wearing
a bobble hat that
matched his smart
uniform.

"We're here to
see the queen," said
Rachel.

"You will find
her in the palace

gardens with Alyssa the Snow Queen Fairy," he said. "Stanley will show you where they are."

He snapped his fingers, and Stanley, a young frog footman who the girls had met once before, came hurrying to their side.

"Hello again, Stanley," said Kirsty.

Stanley smiled and bowed.

"Welcome back to the palace," he said. "Please follow me and I will take you to the queen."

Feeling excited, Rachel and Kirsty fluttered along behind him. As they entered the palace gardens, they both gasped and stopped. A snowy slope had just curved over the top of a hedge towards them, as thin as a ribbon. It zigzagged around them, then looped over the Seeing Pool and disappeared into the maze.

"That looks like the best fun," said Jayda longingly. "If only I had my board."

"Sorry," called a laughing voice. "I almost didn't see you there."

Alyssa the Snow Queen Fairy appeared from behind the hedge.

"Hi, Alyssa," said Rachel. "It's lovely to see you again."

Alyssa hugged both Rachel and Kirsty.

"I'm here to build a few ski runs for the Snow Fun Day," she said.

"You're doing a magnificent job," said a kind, warm voice.

Queen Titania was gliding towards them across the snow. She was wearing a raspberry-red robe, trimmed with white velvet. Rachel and Kirsty curtsied.

"Welcome to Fairyland, dear friends," said the queen. "The Gold Medal Games Fairies have told me how much you have done to help them. I know that you are going to do everything you can to save Jayda's magical snowboard. Is there anything that I can do to help?"

Rachel and Kirsty thought hard. Then

Rachel remembered how jealous Jack Frost had been when everyone was admiring Kim's snowboarding skills that morning, and an idea popped into her head.

"There is one thing, Your Majesty," she said. "Jack Frost is causing trouble because he wants to be a star. He wants everyone to be watching him and admiring his amazing tricks. But what if he could do that at the Snow Fun Day?"

"But the Snow Fun Day has no winners," said the queen. "It is about enjoying the sports, not winning."

"I thought that if Jack Frost could be the guest performer, he would feel so special that he would forget about the Gold Medal Games," said Rachel.

The queen's eyes twinkled.

"What a good idea," she said. "Jack Frost is very proud. When he feels special, he sometimes behaves better."

Queen Titania waved her wand, and the snow in front of her began to shiver. It hardened and thickened into the shape of a snowboard. The queen drew a blue lightning bolt in mid air. It sank down and settled onto the hardened snow. Finally, the queen wrote the words 'Lightning Frost' in silver lettering. The finished snowboard rose out

of the snow and hovered in front of them.

"It's beautiful," said Jayda in a whisper.

With another wave of the queen's wand, a scroll of paper appeared, with a golden seal.

"This is a royal invitation for Jack Frost, asking him to be our guest of honour," said Queen Titania.

Jayda took the board and the scroll.

"I'll send you back to your afternoon lesson with Kim," Jayda said. "You need to learn about jumping so that you can have the most fun in the competition tomorrow. I'll be there, and we'll see if we can persuade Jack Frost to do the right thing and give me my board back."

Chapter Five
Snowball Surprise

The morning light poured into Rachel and Kirsty's chalet bedroom. They yawned, stretched and groaned.

"Ouch, my poor legs ache so much," said Kirsty, laughing and rubbing them. "It must be all the snowboarding we did yesterday afternoon."

"I loved learning to jump," said Rachel. "The best thing was the feeling when you come off the ground. I just kept forgetting to bend my knees."

"Loads of people were forgetting things," said Kirsty. "It must be because of Jack Frost. Have you decided what trick you're going to do in your jump today?"

"I'm going to try a nose grab," said Rachel. "I just have to remember to touch the front of the board. But unless we get Jayda's board back, I'll forget everything."

"So will everyone," said Kirsty. "It's going to be really hard to get it away from Jack Frost. He never leaves it alone."

Rachel went over to the window and opened it, leaning out and breathing the crisp, cold air.

"What if my plan fails?" she asked in a small voice.

Kirsty came to stand beside her.

"I think your plan is brilliant," she said in a firm voice. "Besides – oh my goodness – move!"

She pushed Rachel back as a snowball soared through the window and smashed into the rug. Jayda was sitting in the middle of the fast-melting snow.

"Good morning," she said, laughing. "Now that was fun. I think I'll travel by snowball more often."

She stood up and shook the snow off herself. The snowboard and the queen's message for Jack Frost were under her arm.

"I was hoping to be in time for breakfast," she added with a grin. "Chalet breakfasts are the best."

"Fly into my pocket," said Rachel. "I'll slip you some fresh croissant."

After breakfast, Rachel, Kirsty and the other competitors went to the board park. It was looking very different today. There were lots of spectators, and a press area where the journalists could ask the competitors questions.

"Look," said Rachel, touching Kirsty's

arm. "Jack Frost is talking to the press."

He was strutting up and down in front of the cameras and microphones, boasting about what a great snowboarder he was. Jayda's snowboard was under his arm.

"He thinks we're out of the way," said
Kirsty. "Come on, let's try to talk to him."

They walked up behind him.

"Excuse me?" said Rachel politely.

Jack Frost whirled around and gawped
at the girls.

"What are you
doing here?" he
hissed. "You're
supposed to be
fairy sized *and in
my hat*."

Rachel's mouth
was dry with
nervousness.

"We've got a suggestion," she said. "You
could go to the fairies' Snow Fun Day
and–"

"I'm not going to a stupid fun day!"

Jack Frost snarled at them. "Leave me alone. You can't stop me. I'm going to win the final gold medal, and no one apart from me will ever win it again."

Kirsty tried to say something, but Jack Frost was already walking away. Rachel groaned.

"I've ruined it," she said miserably. "He's keeping the board and it's all my fault."

"Don't be so hard on yourself," said Jayda from inside Rachel's pocket. "I know your plan will work. We need to find somewhere away from the crowds so that I can show him the snowboard and the invitation."

Kirsty gave her best friend a quick hug.

"Jayda's right," she said. "Let's follow Jack Frost and find a quiet space."

There were people everywhere. The fence around the board park was lined with crowds of spectators, and cameras were clicking and whirring in all directions. Then Kirsty spotted something.

"The resort map," she whispered.

The main map of Dewbelle's slopes was set onto a huge wooden panel, taller than a grown-up. There was a little overhang roof jutting out above the map to protect

it from the weather. When the girls walked behind it, they were hidden from the cameras and the crowds.

"It's big enough for all of us," said Rachel. "But how are we going to get Jack Frost to come over here?"

"Leave that to me," said Jayda.

Chapter Six
The Big Air

Jayda popped her head out of Rachel's pocket and tapped her wand on her own mouth. Then she spoke into her cupped hand, and the girls gasped. As she spoke the first word, it turned into a tiny flake of snow.

"There is a special gift for the best

snowboarder in the land behind the resort map," she said.

The word-snowflakes floated into her cupped hand. She took a deep breath and blew them like a kiss. Kirsty and Rachel peeped around the map and saw the snowflakes dance across the snow to land on Jack Frost's ear.

"As the flakes melt, he'll hear the words," Jayda explained.

Jack Frost turned eagerly and looked at the map.

"It's working!" said Rachel.

Jayda dropped the snowboard and the invitation out of Rachel's pocket. With a wave of her wand, they grew to human size. Jack Frost came hurrying around the map and stopped in his tracks.

"Oh, it's you," he grumbled.

He half turned to leave, and then spotted the snowboard.

"This is a gift from Queen Titania," said Rachel.

"And this is a message," Kirsty added, handing him the tightly wound scroll with its golden seal.

Jack Frost opened the invitation and read it. His eyes widened.

"The guest of honour?" he murmured.

"You would be the star of the day," said Kirsty. "Every fairy would be watching."

"Brooke the Photographer Fairy has offered to take some special pictures of you," added Jayda.

"You'd be more important than the gold medal winner," Rachel added. "You'd be like Kim, with everyone cheering you on."

"All you have to do is swap Jayda's board for this one with your name on it," said Kirsty.

Jack Frost's mouth twitched and twisted for a moment. Then a big, beaming smile broke out. He shoved Jayda's board towards the girls and snatched the one that the queen had made.

"It's a deal," he said.

There was a flash of blue lightning, and he was gone. The girls heaved sighs of relief, and Jayda fluttered out of Rachel's pocket and touched her snowboard. At once, it shrank to fairy size.

"It's good to see you again, old friend," she said, patting the board.

"Gold medal competitors, please come to the board park," boomed a voice. "The snowboarding competition is about to begin."

"We have to go," said Kirsty. "Goodbye, Jayda."

"Goodbye, girls, and thank you," said Jayda with a warm smile. "Because of you, the gold medal competition will be a success and I can join in with the Snow Fun Day in Fairyland."

"Everyone's a winner," said Rachel.

Jayda gave them a little wave, then tucked her wand into her helmet and disappeared in a flurry of glittering fairy dust. Rachel and Kirsty raced back to the board park, found their snowboards and joined their friends for the big air.

Lenny was the first to compete. The

crowd roared when he twirled all the
way around during his jump and landed
without a wobble.

"A fantastic 360!" yelled the
commentator.

Rachel remembered her nose grab, and Kirsty's tail grab got a round of applause. Doing the jumps was fun, but it was even better watching their friends on the slope while sharing warm croissants from the bakery together.

At last, everyone had performed and the head judge stood up to reveal the winner.

"You have all been magnificent," she said. "But the clear champion was Lenny of Allenross Academy!"

The crowd went wild with whistles and cheers. Rachel and Kirsty whooped and clapped as he collected his medal.

"As this is the last event of the Gold Medal Games, we have a little gift for you," said the judge.

"Everyone will get a hoodie with their names and events printed on. Tonight there will be a disco at the ice rink. Until then, have fun in the snow!"

Rachel and Kirsty lined up to get their hoodies, which were red with white lettering.

"There's something in the pouch of mine," said Rachel.

"Mine too," said Kirsty.

Each of them pulled out a little keyring with a picture in a tiny silver frame. It showed Jack Frost at the centre of a crowd of smiling fairies. He was holding his snowboard and beaming with pride. Queen Titania and King Oberon were standing at his side. On the back of the keyring were the words: *Snow Fun Day Souvenir*.

"Dewbelle really is the best resort in Silverlake Valley," said Rachel.

"I don't think this adventure could have had a happier ending," said Kirsty. "Even Jack Frost's dreams came true!"

The End

**Now it's time for Kirsty and
Rachel to help...**

Elizabeth the Jubilee Fairy

Read on for a sneak peek...

"The Sovereign's Sceptre," Kirsty read
out, staring wide-eyed at the glass case
in front of her. Inside was a long golden
sceptre with a diamond cross on top.
Below the cross was an enormous, pear-
shaped diamond that glowed in the lights.
"Rachel, isn't that *amazing*?"

"Amazing!" Rachel agreed. She was
completely dazzled by all the Crown
Jewels on display – the crowns, the
sceptres, the orbs and the rings.

The girls were visiting the Tower of
London with their parents, and they'd
enjoyed seeing the Yeoman Warders in

their colourful costumes and the big black ravens who lived inside the walls of the Tower. Then they had queued to see the Crown Jewels, along with hundreds of other tourists. Later, they were going to join the crowds gathering on the banks of the River Thames to watch the start of the queen's Diamond Jubilee celebrations. The girls could hardly wait!

"What does the guidebook say, Dad?" Rachel asked.

Mr Walker consulted his book. "The sceptre was made for King Charles the Second, and our present queen carried it when she was crowned at Westminster Abbey sixty years ago," he replied.

"It looks heavy!" Rachel said.

"And is that a *real* diamond?" Kirsty

asked, staring at the huge, glittering stone in awe.

"Yes, it's called the Great Star of Africa," Mr Walker explained. "It's one of nine diamonds cut from the Cullinan Diamond, which is the largest that's ever been found."

Read Elizabeth the Jubilee Fairy to
find out what adventures are in store for Kirsty and Rachel!

Read the brand-new series
from Daisy Meadows...

Ride. Dream. Believe.

Meet best friends Aisha and Emily
and journey to the secret world of
Enchanted Valley!

Calling all parents, carers and teachers!
The Rainbow Magic fairies are here to help
your child enter the magical world of reading.
Whatever reading stage they are at, there's
a Rainbow Magic book for everyone!
Here is Lydia the Reading Fairy's guide to
supporting your child's journey at all levels.

(1)

Starting Out

Our Rainbow Magic Beginner Readers are perfect for first-time readers who are just beginning to develop reading skills and confidence. Approved by teachers, they contain a full range of educational levelling, as well as lively full-colour illustrations.

(2)

Developing Readers

Rainbow Magic Early Readers contain longer stories and wider vocabulary for building stamina and growing confidence. These are adaptations of our most popular Rainbow Magic stories, specially developed for younger readers in conjunction with an Early Years reading consultant, with full-colour illustrations.

(3)

Going Solo

The Rainbow Magic chapter books - a mixture of series and one-off specials - contain accessible writing to encourage your child to venture into reading independently. These highly collectible and much-loved magical stories inspire a love of reading to last a lifetime.

www.orchardseriesbooks.co.uk

"Rainbow Magic got my daughter reading chapter books. Great sparkly covers, cute fairies and traditional stories full of magic that she found impossible to put down" - Mother of Edie (6 years)

"Florence LOVES the Rainbow Magic books. She really enjoys reading now" - Mother of Florence (6 years)

Read along the Reading Rainbow!

Well done – you have completed the book!

This book was worth 1 star.

See how far you have climbed on the Reading Rainbow opposite.
The more books you read, the more stars you can colour in
and the closer you will be to becoming a Royal Fairy!

Do you want to print your own Reading Rainbow?

1) Go to the Rainbow Magic website

2) Download and print out the poster

3) Colour in a star for every book you finish
and climb the Reading Rainbow

4) For every step up the rainbow,
you can download your very own certificate

There's all this and lots more at
orchardseriesbooks.co.uk

You'll find activities, stories, a special newsletter
AND you can search for the fairy with your name!